Dear Reader,

Have you ever told a little white lie? We all do it from time to time. Most of us get away with it without being found out. Most of us. ☺ Not so Juliet Montague in my prequel to The Chatsfield continuity.

Juliet is invited to a posh weekend hen's party at the super glamorous Chatsfield Hotel in London. Desperate to fit into the sophisticated clique of Kendra's Clan, she invents a fiancé so she isn't the only girl without an engagement ring on her finger. Which would have been perfectly fine if her big brother's best friend, Marcus Bainbridge, hadn't turned up in person!

I hope you enjoy *Engaged at The Chatsfield,* where the doors of The Chatsfield Hotel are open for the first time for you to see what's coming ahead. Watch out for cameo appearances by notorious bad boy Lucca Chatsfield and, of course, the steely-eyed CEO Christos Giatrakos!

Writing this prequel and Book Two—*Playboy's Lesson*—were *sooo* much fun it was the highlight of my year.

I hope reading The Chatsfield continuity will be a highlight of yours.

Warmest wishes,

Melanie Milburne

From as soon as **Melanie Milburne** could pick up a pen she knew she wanted to write. It was when she picked up her first Harlequin Mills & Boon® book at seventeen that she realized she wanted to write romance. Distracted for a few years by meeting and marrying her own handsome hero, surgeon husband Steve, and having two boys, plus completing a master's of education and becoming a nationally ranked athlete (masters swimming), she decided to write. Five submissions later she sold her first book and is now a multipublished, award-winning *USA TODAY* bestselling author. In 2008 she won the Australian Romance Readers Association's most popular category/series romance, and in 2011 she won the prestigious Romance Writers of Australia R*BY Award.

Melanie loves to hear from her readers via her website, www.melaniemilburne.com.au, or on Facebook.

Other titles by Melanie Milburne available in ebook:

AT NO MAN'S COMMAND
PLAYBOY'S LESSON
  (The Chatsfield)
NEVER GAMBLE WITH A CAFFARELLI
  (Those Scandalous Caffarellis)
NEVER UNDERESTIMATE A CAFFARELLI
  (Those Scandalous Caffarellis)

Melanie Milburne

Engaged at The Chatsfield

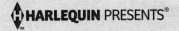 HARLEQUIN PRESENTS®

Recycling programs
for this product may
not exist in your area.

ISBN-13: 978-0-373-20261-4

ENGAGED AT THE CHATSFIELD

Copyright © 2014 by Harlequin Books S.A.

Special thanks and acknowledgment are given to
Melanie Milburne for her contribution to The Chatsfield series.

www.Harlequin.com

To Christine Kiernan,
who grooms my poodles, Polly and Lily.
Thank you for being such a wonderful support to my
little babies and for being such a beautiful person. xx

CHAPTER ONE

How MANY CALORIES are there in a caramel-swirl cupcake? Juliet typed into her smartphone on the way to the Chatsfield Hotel for a hen's party high tea. *Oh no!* She bit her lip as she typed in a chocolate éclair and then a macaroon. *Double oh no!* And that wasn't counting the champagne cocktails Kendra Ashford would have flowing like...well, like champagne.

Juliet typed again. Groaned again. The smoked salmon pinwheels and sausage rolls were not much better. A weekend of this and she would have to nibble lettuce leaves and drink wheatgrass shakes for a month. Probably two.

But it would be worth it, because for forty-eight hours she would finally be part of the In Group. She would no longer be on the fringe where the less popular and less trendy were shunted. She would be part of Kendra's Clan: the posse of pampered heiresses who partied at all the right places with all the right people.

She would belong.... Even though she was not an heiress and she couldn't remember the last time she had been to a party...unless you counted the first birthday for her neighbour's little boy, Haseem, three weeks ago, where she had baked the cake—a teddy-bear-shaped one—because his mum had been too sick with the flu to make it for him.

Juliet walked into the swish foyer of the hotel. Crystal chandeliers overhead threw bright prisms of light over the polished marble floor. The air was filled with the scent of fresh peonies and roses and lilies from a giant and artfully arranged bouquet in the centre of the area.

The recent appointment of a new CEO at the Chatsfield had brought about some major changes to the hotel brand, and already they showed and glowed. Everyone wanted to be seen at the sparkling new hot spot in town. High tea at the London Chatsfield was now a premier event with parties having to book months in advance. Cocktails in the bar where the rich and famous gathered before they dined in the restaurant took sipping drinks and fine dining to a whole new level of decadence.

The Chatsfield signature colours of blue and gold had been totally revamped with plush new velvet and silk furnishings, and when you added the smartly uniformed and attentive staff members, who were intent on giving professional and yet personalised service, the hotel had the atmosphere of a royal palace.

The new broom, Christos Giantrakos, was implementing marketing initiatives, programs and codes of accountability that were rumoured to be causing shockwaves amongst the Chatsfield siblings. Christos was known in corporate circles to be a take-no-prisoners type who would not tolerate freeloaders or timewasters.

The paparazzi were on permanent call outside the hotel in anticipation of a showdown with Lucca Chatsfield, one of the twin sons, who was known around town as an idle playboy who lived only to party.

The foyer was buzzing with activity as people checked in and out. Juliet moved forward in the queue and collected her swipe key with assurances from the smiling attendant that her luggage would be sent to her room directly.

Welcome to Kendra Ashford and Her Bachelorette Party Guests was written in gold copperplate on an antique brass notice board. It made Juliet feel like Cinderella gate-crashing the ball. She wasn't sure why Kendra had sent her the invitation. Well, that wasn't strictly true. Juliet's older brother, Benedict, had just finished filming the lead role in a Hollywood romantic comedy, which was already causing a stir amongst the critics and mentions of an Oscar Award.

Suddenly she was being invited to *everyone's* parties.

The maid of honour, Harriet Penhallon, came teetering towards Juliet surrounded by a cloud of exotic perfume. It didn't look like Harriet's pretty floral designer tea-party dress was pinching her under the armpits or squeezing her around the waist, and her sky-high heels definitely weren't giving her hammertoes. Harriet looked as though she had just stepped off a photo shoot with her immaculate makeup and perfectly coiffed hair.

Juliet felt like a basset hound turning up at a pedigree poodle show.

'You're the last one to arrive.' Harriet's gaze swept over Juliet's retro dress. 'Wow, don't you look nice?'

Juliet knew that was code for "You look like a fat sow," but she smiled anyway and sucked her tummy in a little harder. 'Sorry, am I late? I had to change trains because of a breakdown on the line.'

'No, we don't kick off high tea till half-three.' Harriet glanced at her watch. 'That gives you thirty-two minutes to freshen up and change.' She gave a smile that wouldn't look out of place on an orthodontist's website home page. 'If you're lucky you might even get a glimpse of Lucca Chatsfield. He arrived a few minutes ago. I just got a tweet about it. He's staying the weekend.'

'Not for Kendra's hen party, I take it?'

Harriet laughed. 'No, but I wouldn't say no to him doing a little striptease show for us, would you?'

Juliet hated that she blushed so readily. It made her appear as naive and gauche as she felt. Newsfeeds and social media buzzed constantly with Lucca Chatsfield's latest shenanigans. Not that she moved in the circles he stirred. She didn't have a circle…apart from one of loneliness. Her job as a library-based rare book expert was her dream career, but it made for a pretty quiet social life.

'I'm sure he's very attractive, but I prefer intelligence over looks,' she said, immediately thinking of Ben's best friend since childhood, Marcus Bainbridge. But then, she thought of him a lot. Too much. Way, way too much. It was a bit of an obsession she had developed since Christmas, when he had joined Ben and their mother in Bath instead of dividing his time between his bitterly divorced parents and their new partners and families.

Aloof and reserved, which most people mistook for arrogance, Marcus was a perfect counterpoint to Ben's outgoing daredevil personality. He'd been like a second older brother to Juliet since she was ten, when he had fixed a puncture on her bike because Ben, at sixteen, had been too busy chatting up his latest conquest.

But last Christmas something had changed.

It had been the first time they'd been alone together since The Incident. Her eighteenth birthday party. *Blush.* Too much alcohol. *Double blush.* Cornering Marcus in the study. *Cringe.* Him politely but firmly rejecting her clumsy advances. Him sternly lecturing her on the dangers of excessive drinking. *Cringe. Blush. Cringe.*

He had avoided her ever since.

Until last Christmas…

Six months on and she remembered as if it were yesterday. They had been washing up after lunch while her mother made a phone call to an elderly relative and Ben talked to his agent in L.A. Marcus handed her a wineglass to dry and her fingers brushed against his as she took it from him. Their gazes collided. Meshed. Stilled. *Heated.*

A sensation like a fizzing electrical pulse travelled from his fingers to hers, raced all the way up her arm and then through her body to light a fire in her core. She saw the flare of his pupils, the way they made his eyes darken to a midnight blue. The way his fingers didn't jerk away, but lingered. Burned against hers.

His gaze went to her mouth. Paused there. Her lips felt scorched from the heat of his gaze. She heard the scuff of his shoe on the tiled floor as he closed the half-step distance between their bodies....

But then Ben came bounding in to announce he had got the part for the rom-com. Champagne was opened. Toasts and celebrations were conducted. There were no more private moments. Marcus kept his distance. Business as usual.

'So—' Harriet smoothed an imaginary hair behind her ear. It was a ploy Juliet knew was so Harriet could showcase her glittering and ridiculously huge and brand new—as of last week—diamond engagement ring. 'Are you seeing anyone?'

Juliet was going to say no. Of course she was. Why wouldn't she say no? She hadn't dated anyone since Simon Foster had made a fool out of her five years ago, stringing her along for months with weekend dates while he got it on in the city with a size-zero blonde the rest of the time. Of course she was going to say no. Her mouth even went as far to shape the word but instead she said, 'N-yes.'

Harriet's impeccably groomed eyebrows shot up beneath her perfectly trimmed and blow-dried fringe. 'Who is it?' But before Juliet could think of a name, Harriet had already come up with one. 'It's Marcus, isn't it? That stuck-up naval architect friend of your brother's?'

'He's not stuck up.' Had she sounded *too* defensive?

'Oh. My. God.' Harriet's china-blue eyes were as round as the satellite dishes on the International Space Station. 'Get outta here. Are you serious? Marcus Bainbridge and *you*?'

Juliet's back came up at Harriet's incredulity. She knew she wasn't beautiful—or at least not without soft lighting or a quick touch-up in Photoshop. She knew she didn't have the best figure, and she hated her freckles because they made her look about eight years old. But was it *that* unbelievable that a man like Marcus would be interested in her? He had *almost* kissed her at Christmas. She hadn't been imagining that. *Had she?*

She was tired of being the odd one out.

Tired of being almost twenty-nine years old and unattached. The only one of Kendra's Clan who was still single. An object of pity. Like at school, where she had been the only girl in her class without a father. The bookish nerd who studied instead of dated. The lonely fringe-dweller who had a sudden rush of best friends around exam time when everyone wanted her to help them swot.

What would it hurt to pretend she belonged to someone? It was only for the weekend. She could head back to Bath on Monday morning and no one would be the wiser. It wasn't as if Marcus would even hear about it; he was currently living in Dubai while he designed a luxury yacht for a sheikh.

'Yes,' she said, and took it one step further because she didn't care for the way Harriet was still gaping at her. 'It's serious.'

'*How* serious? Has he asked you to marry him?' Harriet glanced at Juliet's left hand, her eyes narrowing. 'You're not wearing an engagement ring.'

Juliet curled her fingers into a ball. There was a jeweller's store half a block from the hotel. She had stopped to gaze dreamily at the rings in the window on her way past. 'Erm, well, no, not yet. But I'm picking it up. Soon. This afternoon. Before tea.' *What are you doing? Are you crazy?*

'You'd better get a wriggle on,' Harriet said. 'I want everyone assembled for when Kendra makes her entrance. I want everything to be perfect for her.'

'Don't worry.' Juliet pasted a smile on her face. 'It will be.'

CHAPTER TWO

MARCUS WAS JETLAGGED and hungry and a tension headache was throbbing like a pneumatic drill behind his eyeballs as the cab pulled up outside the Chatsfield in London. He still had some work to do on his proposal for Gene Chatsfield's luxury yacht before he presented it on Monday morning. He was one of three naval architects shortlisted to pitch for the multimillion-pound contract. It would be a career coup if he pulled it off, especially on the back of his success with the Dubai deal. He figured staying in-house might give him the edge on his competitors. It would demonstrate his commitment and dedication to the Chatsfield brand. He had heard the newly appointed CEO, Christos Giantrakos, was a stickler for that sort of thing.

Marcus paid the driver and turned to enter the hotel just as a small figure came bolting down the brass steps from the other direction. Her shiny brown-haired head was bent down as she glanced at her watch, a little pleat of a frown was pulling at her brow and her teeth were savaging her lower lip.

'Juliet?'

It was as if an invisible wall had come down in front of her. She stopped dead. Froze. Then she slowly turned to face him. For a moment her face was as white as the polka dots on her cute retro dress, but then her cheeks went as cherry-red as the background fabric. 'M-Marcus?' Her voice came out like a squeak.

'You're staying here?' he asked.

The tip of her tongue swept over her lips in a darting movement. 'Erm…yes.' Her throat moved up and down. 'Y-you?'

He gave her a self-deprecating smile. 'I just flew in from Dubai. Can't you tell?'

Her toffee-brown eyes moved over his rumpled clothes and unshaven jaw before meshing with his gaze. She seemed to be having trouble speaking. Her creamy throat kept moving up and down as if something was lodged there.

'Are you okay?'

'F-fine.' She smiled a smile that didn't quite reach her eyes. 'How long are you—' she gave another tight-looking swallow '—staying?'

'Just for the weekend,' he said. 'I have an appointment with Gene Chatsfield, the owner, and his CEO first thing Monday. I'm pitching for a design project. What about you?'

She shifted her weight from foot to foot, the fingers of her right hand fiddling with the strap of her handbag. The afternoon light caught something glittering on her left hand before she tucked it out of sight.

Something grabbed at his chest like a claw. Tightened. Squeezed.

Juliet was engaged?

Why hadn't Ben given him the heads-up? He didn't know she'd been seeing anyone. Last Christmas he thought… What had he thought? He *hadn't* been thinking. He'd acted on impulse. Something he never did. He blamed it on the glasses of wine at lunch, the eggnog and the brandy butter. It must have gone to his head. His chest gave another suffocating spasm. The thought of her dating…*having sex* with some guy made his insides feel hollow and empty, as if they had been scraped out with something sharp.

'Hen's party,' she said.

'Your own?'

She looked at him blankly for a moment. 'No…Kendra Ashford's.'

Marcus had never understood what Juliet saw in the clique of girls who called themselves Kendra's Clan. A bunch of pampered aristocrats who did nothing but preen and party, usually with the paparazzi around to document it. Not that he could necessarily talk, given his father's ridiculous wealth, but at least he didn't brandish it about. *And* he worked for a living. He couldn't see how Juliet had anything in common with them, but she'd been at boarding school with them, and she was a loyal little thing and wouldn't hear a bad word said about anyone.

He pointed to the ring on her finger, trying to ignore the painful ache in his chest. 'Who's the lucky guy?'

Two spots of colour spread even further over her cheeks making her cute freckles stand out like a dusting of cinnamon sugar on the top of a teacake. 'Erm…'

She did that foot shuffling, weight shifting thing again, reminding him of when she was ten years old and embarrassed about asking him to help her change the tyre on her pushbike.

Back then the six years difference in their age had seemed like a generation. Even at eighteen she had been far too young—rather memorably demonstrated by her gauche attempt to kiss him in the study the night of her birthday party. He had always made sure he was never alone with her after that, especially if there was alcohol around. She didn't have much of a head for it. Not that *he* could talk given what almost happened at Christmas.

Now it was…it was a surprise to realise how grown up she was. Grown up enough to get engaged.

His chest seized again.

To get married.

He hadn't noticed quite *how* grown up she was until last Christmas. In the past she had always been his best mate's kid sister. He hadn't seen her as anything else. He hadn't allowed himself to, especially after the incident in the study. Getting involved with his best friend's baby sister was breaking a strict code of mateship. If things didn't work out, it got messy for everyone. He had too much respect for Ben and his mother, Grace—not to mention Juliet herself—to take any risks in that area.

But last Christmas…

Marcus pushed the thought back. Best not to go there. She belonged to someone else now. He tried to ignore the sinking sensation in the pit of his stomach. He hoped it was someone who was worthy of her. She was a decent girl. A sweet and caring soul who could easily get trampled on or taken advantage of because she wasn't street smart or sophisticated. But that's what he liked about her. She was intelligent and kind, not shallow and vacuous and self-serving like some of the women her big brother was currently hanging out with in L.A. 'So, is it anyone I know?' he asked.

The point of her tongue came out again and moistened her soft Cupid's bow mouth. Her cheeks were so red now he could have cooked a couple of rounds of toast on them. 'I didn't think you'd turn up like this,' she said. 'Ben didn't tell me you were due back...'

'Yeah, well, I'm lucky to get a word from your brother now he's so rich and famous,' he said. 'Last time I heard from him was about a month ago. He texted me a photo of himself on a red carpet somewhere surrounded by Hollywood starlets.'

She did the lip chew thing again. 'He's certainly got an awful lot of friends now....'

Marcus's gut clenched as if a fist had grabbed at his intestines. Was Juliet involved with some guy who only wanted her for a connection to her famous brother? Some sleazy status-seeker who wanted to fast-track his own career in show business? She was so innocent and guileless she mightn't see past the superficial charm. Why hadn't Ben warned her?

'Well, well, well, if it isn't Romeo himself.'

Marcus looked up to see Harriet Penhallon, one of Kendra's Clan, coming towards them with a smirk on her face. 'Congratulations, Marcus,' Harriet said, eyeing him up and down like an auctioneer does at a cattle market. 'Who would have thought?'

Who would have thought what? Marcus opened his mouth to say it out loud when he heard Juliet make a strangled sound beside him. He glanced down at her with a frown. 'What's wrong?'

Her brown eyes had never looked bigger. Wider. The pupils like dark pools of rippling panic. He even heard her take a gulp. 'I told Harriet…erm…that I… that we…erm…'

'Told Harriet what?'

'That you're engaged,' Harriet said.

Marcus blinked. *Engaged?* Juliet was pretending she was engaged…*to him?* What was she thinking? What was going on? Why would she do such a thing? He'd been sick with worry that she'd been seduced by some creep, only to find it was all a game of charades. He didn't have time for such nonsense, damn it. What a waste of angst. He was supposed to be here on business. He wasn't here to play silly schoolgirl games. His professional reputation was under the spotlight. Not his personal life. Not that he had one right now.

He looked down at her again. Her expression was a mixture of contrition and hope. Hope he wouldn't blow her cover? Publicly embarrass her by denying it? Was she doing this to get social cache with her so-called friends? Surely she'd known he would find out one way or the other. No one could do or say anything these days without someone tweeting or texting about it. There was no such thing as local gossip these days. The whole planet found out in a matter of seconds.

But if he contradicted her, it would make her look foolish in front of her friends. It might draw even more attention to him than he wanted right now. It wasn't such a leap to think they might be an item. He'd been a part of her family for years.

Besides, he didn't care for the narrow-eyed look on Harriet Penhallon's face.

'Yes…that's right, so we are.' He put an arm around Juliet and brought her close to his body. She felt soft and warm and feminine and smelt of summer flowers—sweet peas with a hint of orange blossom. Exotic and yet old fashioned and touchingly familiar. 'We were going to keep it a secret for a little while longer, weren't we, sweetie?'

Juliet looked up at him with a faltering smile. 'I'm sorry…'

Not as much as you're going to be, he thought. What the hell was she playing at? *Engaged?* Hell's bells. What was Ben going to make of this? 'It's fine, darling.' He mentally ground his teeth. 'It had to come out sooner or later.'

Harriet put a hand over her mouth in a theatrical manner. 'Oops. I didn't realise you hadn't officially announced it. I just tweeted it to all Kendra's followers.' She dropped her hand and smiled broadly. 'All five hundred and fifty thousand of them.'

CHAPTER THREE

JULIET COULDN'T LOOK at Marcus. She wanted to die. She wanted the ground to open up and swallow her whole and spit her out on the other side of the world. She wanted to be someone else. Someone who had a *real* fiancé, not a pretend one. She didn't want to be the last girl Marcus would ever think of being involved with, let alone engaged to.

She could tell he was angry. He was too polite to show it, but she knew him well enough to know he was absolutely furious. She could hear his jaw working and his teeth grinding like a saw. His arm was still around her, a warm band of strength that was as tense as a wire. Even through the layer of her cotton dress she could feel every corded muscle, every lean sinew, all of his latent strength and physical power. His hand was on her right hip, the searing touch of his fingers burning through her body like a brand.

She had never been this close to him before. Close enough to feel the long, tall, athletic frame of him. Close enough to smell his lemon-based aftershave with its grace note of lime. At six foot three, he towered over her but somehow she fit snugly against him. Her body quivered at the contact. She could feel the electric heat coursing through her as if his sensual energy was powering up hers.

'Gotta run,' Harriet said as she gave them a fingertip wave. 'Don't be late, Juliet. We can't start tea without you.'

Juliet stepped out of Marcus's hold as soon as Harriet had disappeared inside the hotel. 'I can explain—'

'Mr Bainbridge?' A person holding a camera with a telephoto lens approached from the other side of Marcus. Other people with cameras and tripods were close behind; moving towards them like a pack of strangely shaped black-and-grey insects.

'How does it feel to be engaged to Hollywood's new heartthrob Benedict Montague's little sister?' the first journalist asked.

'Can we have the first official portrait?' a second photographer asked.

'Is it true you've known Ben since he was eight years old?' a third asked. 'That you knew him before he was famous?'

Marcus reached for Juliet's hand, his fingers closing over hers so firmly she felt her prop engagement ring bite into her flesh. 'We have no comment to make. Please excuse us. This is a private moment and we wish to be left alone to enjoy it.'

Juliet could just imagine what Marcus was going to say when he got her alone, so she was all up for hanging out with the paparazzi for as long as she could. She smiled at the gathered cameramen and -women. 'A photo? Of course! Where would you like us to stand? Here?' She shuffled into position, dragging Marcus with her. 'Smile, darling. Isn't this fun? I've always wanted to be famous. Just wait till I tell Ben we've upstaged him.'

The cameras flashed a few rounds but as soon as a journalist pushed a recording device towards Marcus his rictus smile fell away. 'That's it, folks. Time to move on.'

All but marching Juliet into the hotel, Marcus spoke out of the side of his tautly held mouth as if spitting out bitter-tasting pellets. 'Are you out of your mind? What the hell is going on?'

Juliet kept her smile in place as a cameraman had followed them into the hotel to capture a shot of Lucca Chatsfield, who was heading to the bar with a bevy of beautiful women surrounding him like groupies around a rock star. 'Look, darling,' she said. 'Don't you think he's gorgeous? No wonder he's got all those women trailing after him. I've heard he's really charming, too. Maybe you could introduce me to him since you know his father.'

Marcus glowered at her. 'Just you wait until I get you alone, young lady.'

Juliet didn't have to pretend to shiver in anticipation. It was for real. She hadn't realised how heart-stoppingly handsome he was when he was het up. He was always so cool and in control. So polite and formal and aloof. But underneath that cool reserve was a man with strong feelings and emotions. With hot-blooded passion.

A Chatsfield staff member came over to them with

a sycophantic smile. 'Miss Montague, you should have told us who you were when you checked in,' he said. 'We didn't know you were the sister of a Hollywood movie star. We've upgraded you and Mr Bainbridge to one of our deluxe suites specially designed for affianced couples. The champagne is complimentary, of course.'

Juliet could practically hear Marcus's eyes rolling into the back of his head. 'Oh, you shouldn't have done that.' She tried to disguise a flutter of panic. This was getting so out of hand it was farcical. He was going to *strangle* her for this.

'Thank you.' Marcus gripped her hand even tighter. 'It's much appreciated.'

Once they had been given their swipe card keys, Marcus led Juliet by the elbow to the bank of elevators. 'Don't say a word.'

'I can ex—'

He pushed a finger against her lips. 'Not. One. Word.'

Juliet tasted the sweat and salt of his fingertip as she ran her tongue over her lips while the elevator climbed to their floor. She knew he had a right to be a little cross with her, but surely he would understand once she explained? It wasn't even her fault. Harriet had assumed...

But then she wondered if he was angry because he already had someone in his life.

In his bed.

Her stomach plummeted.

Had he been hooking up with someone here at the hotel?

Had she ruined his rendezvous with a lover? Gate crashed his love life?

Juliet didn't like thinking of him with other women. She knew he had them. He wasn't as much of an out-and-out playboy as Lucca Chatsfield, or even her brother, but he had relationships from time to time. Nothing serious as far as she knew. She suspected he was wary of commitment since his parents' breakup had been so acrimonious and drawn out and so horribly, embarrassingly, horrifyingly public. It was why he loathed the press so much. As a young child he had been dragged into the public brawling match between his parents as they fought for custody.

Marcus would tread very carefully before he selected a wife, if he ever did so. One thing she knew for sure: *it would never be someone like her....*

He opened the door of the suite, where her luggage had already been delivered. There was an ice bucket with a bottle of champagne with a blue-and-gold satin ribbon around its neck and two silver champagne flutes with the Chatsfield *C* engraved on them. A floral arrangement with two red velvet hearts was on the polished sideboard and the king-size bed had two red long-stem roses lying across the snowy-white feather pillows. The new CEO was certainly cracking a very efficient whip around the Chatsfield, Juliet thought.

The door closed with a *snick* and she turned to face Marcus. 'Please don't be cross. I didn't mean—'

'Do you have *any* idea of what you've done? You've

caused a freaking media circus out there. Everyone is tweeting about us like we're reality show celebrities.' He shoved a hand through his hair and muttered a curse as he started pacing the floor. 'If I lose this project because of this, I swear to God I'll—'

'How was I to know you'd turn up?'

He swung around and glared at her so darkly his dark blue eyes looked almost black. 'So, now it's *my* fault, is it? What on earth were you thinking? You'd just let everyone think we were engaged and not tell *me* about it? How were you going to stop it leaking out? Did you think of that?'

She snagged her lower lip again. 'I didn't actually *say* we were engaged. Harriet assumed—'

'You're wearing a bloody engagement ring, for God's sake. Even *I* assumed you were engaged. Little did I know it was to me.'

Juliet winced at his savage look. 'I told her I was seeing someone.'

His brows jammed together. 'Are you?'

Her cheeks grew warm. 'No...'

'So why the charade?'

She fiddled with the clasp on her watch to occupy her hands, otherwise she would have been tempted to wring them in despair. Why was he so disgusted at having his name linked with hers? Was she that much of a toad he couldn't bear the thought of being associated with her romantically? She knew she wasn't a stunning beauty or anything, but she hadn't exactly left a trail of broken mirrors behind her...or at least none that she knew of. 'I told Harriet I was seeing someone and she assumed it was you.'

His frown deepened. 'Why would she assume that?'

Juliet moved over to the sideboard to inspect the floral arrangement rather than let him see how much his comment affronted her. 'I guess because we've been friends for years.'

'There's a heck of a difference between being friends and being engaged.'

She turned from the flowers to look at him again. 'She pressed me for details and when I said it was serious—'

'You told her we were *serious*?'

She raised her chin. 'I'm sorry if the notion disgusts you.'

He gave her a flustered look. 'I'm not— I didn't— Look, don't take it personally. I'm just not looking for a relationship right now. It's the last thing on my mind.'

'I'm not asking you to be in one.' Juliet tried to squash the spreading sense of disappointment that was making her chest feel tight. 'I just wanted to get through this weekend without everyone feeling sorry for me or sniggering at me behind my back because I haven't got a partner. I had no idea Harriet would jump to conclusions so quickly and I certainly had no idea she would send a tweet to all Kendra's followers.'

He swore again. 'Just wait until your brother's followers get wind of it. The whole bloody world will be congratulating us.'

Juliet frowned as she reached for her phone. 'Maybe I should call Mum…'

'Wait.' His hand came down on her arm. The feel of his fingers wrapping around her wrist was like a surge of electricity through her body. She felt it right to her core, to the place his touch had ignited at Christmas. His fingers were warm, broad and strong. She slowly brought her gaze up to his, her stomach dropping like a book toppling off a high shelf as his eyes meshed with hers. 'We need to think this through,' he said. 'We need a plan.'

'A plan?'

His fingers loosened a fraction but he didn't release her. His eyes were dark and unreadable as they held hers. 'Looks like we're stuck with this till the end of the weekend.'

Stuck with me, you mean, Juliet thought with another flicker of resentment. Did he have to make it so flipping obvious? She slipped out of his hold and picked up her purse. 'I have to go to the tea party. We can talk about this later.'

'You do realise we'll have to share this room?'

Juliet's hand froze on the doorknob. She had seen the size of the bed. It was an acre of mattress with a high hedge of pillows. It was big enough to have its own postal code. It was big enough to land a fighter jet on. It was big enough to sleep a football team without any of them touching. Surely she could get through two nights without coming in to contact with him?

She opened the door and sent him her version of a breezy smile. 'I always sleep on the left side of the bed. I hope that's not going to be a problem for you? *Ciao*.'

CHAPTER FOUR

IT WAS A huge problem for Marcus. Right now he couldn't think of a bigger one. He paced the floor like a lion confined in a cat carrier. He had to get through the weekend without compromising his pitch. He had worked so hard to even get shortlisted. Gene Chatsfield was a difficult client, and his brand-new CEO, Christos Giantrakos, even more so. Marcus would have to impress both of them to win the project; swanning around the hotel with the media on his tail was not going to help him. Christos was not the sort of man to tolerate a scandal. Marcus had heard via the grapevine that he was determined to wipe the floor with anyone—including any of the Chatsfield siblings—who dared to bring disrepute or shame on the hotel brand.

But that wasn't the worst of it.

Sharing a room— *sharing a bed*—with Juliet Montague was something Marcus had been fantasizing about since Christmas.

But it was a fantasy, not reality.

She was off limits.

Ben would be furious to think he was having a fling

with his baby sister. They had been best mates since they were at school together. Ben's mum, Grace, was like a surrogate mother to him. The sort of solid and dependable nurturing maternal figure he had needed back in the days when his world had been blown apart by the debacle of his parents' bitter divorce. Grace had provided a safe haven from all the craziness, had listened when he needed to talk, or talked when he needed to listen.

Ben and Juliet's father, Graham Montague, had died of leukaemia when Juliet was a toddler. Like Grace, he studied English Literature at university and their mutual love of Shakespeare had brought them together, hence Juliet and Ben's names. Grace had brought Ben and Juliet up alone since Graham's death and had only recently begun seeing a retired professor of English History in Suffolk.

Ben and Juliet and Grace were Marcus's family. He would do nothing to compromise or break the bond he had with them.

Marcus's phone bleeped and he fished it out of his pocket to see Ben's face come up on the screen. 'Ben, I—'

'Hey, man, I saw this weird tweet about you and Jules getting it on,' Ben said. 'She's not answering her phone. What gives?'

'It's a misunderstanding. It's got blown out of proportion.'

'You're not doing my kid sister, are you?'

Marcus thought of the silky feel of Juliet's skin when he'd wrapped his fingers around her wrist. He thought of last Christmas when her fingers had brushed against his as he'd handed her that glass. He thought of all the nights in between when he had lain in bed wondering what it would be like to kiss that soft pink mouth and draw her curvy little body closer into his arms and—

'Dude?'

Marcus snapped out of his reverie. 'No, of course not. I told you, it's a misunderstanding. Kendra Ashford's having a hen's party here with all her cronies and Juliet was feeling a little left out so she invented a fiancé.'

Ben chuckled. 'And then you showed up. Freaky.'

'I see your sick sense of humour hasn't deserted you.'

'Poor Jules. She must have been beside herself when you appeared like a genie out of a bottle. I hope you weren't too hard on her.'

Remorse tasted sour in Marcus's mouth. He had been brutal to her. Accusing her of setting him up when now, with a bit of reflection, he could see how Harriet would have made her feel pressured. Juliet was too soft when it came to her friends. She was too concerned about fitting in, about pleasing and accommodating everyone. She didn't know how to stand up for herself. She was too trusting and kind and because she always believed the best of everyone; she didn't realise until it was too late when she was being manipulated. 'I'll make it up to her.'

There was a brief silence.

'You know it's kind of cool you're taking care of her for me,' Ben said. 'Mum and I have been worried all this celebrity stuff of mine would make it hard for her to sort out who's genuine and who's not. She's pretty shy when it comes to guys. I don't think she's dated since that jerk did the dirty on her a few years back. Maybe you could show her a good time, help her get back her confidence.'

Marcus frowned. 'You're not telling me to sleep with your sister, are you?'

Ben gave another chuckle. 'You want both your kneecaps, don't you?'

'So tell us how Marcus proposed?' Kendra Ashford said holding out her champagne glass for another re-fill as the waiter came past.

Juliet was feeling a little jazzed from the two drinks she'd consumed—one and a half more than her usual. But the other girls were four or five ahead of her and it was starting to show. The conversation had become more and more risqué as the hen's party accessories had come out. She had never seen drinking straws fash-ioned in the shape of men's genitalia before. Where on earth did they find this stuff? 'Erm…'

'Was it super romantic?' Harriet joined in the con-versation.

'Yes…very.'

'What did he do?' Kendra said. 'Was it as good as Hugh's or Tristan's proposal?'

Juliet took another sip of her cocktail to give herself time to think of a proposal scene. Harriet's and Ken-dra's fiancés had gone to an enormous amount of effort and expense to propose. She didn't want Marcus to look cheap or unromantic in comparison.

But how *would* he propose?

Not that he was ever going to… But hypothetically, if he ever did, how would he do it?

'He called my mother and asked permission first,' she said. 'Then he took me for a candlelit dinner at an exclusive restaurant—'

'Which one?' Harriet asked.

Juliet took another big sip of her drink. This was the reason she never lied. One lie always turned into twenty. 'Oh, we didn't actually *eat* at the restaurant,' she said. 'Marcus ordered a prepacked picnic. We picked it up and then he took me to a private yacht moored on the river. It was one he'd designed for a client. There were candles in those little lantern things hanging from the mast and sails and fairy lights along the deck. There was a string quartet playing and white-suited wait staff and everything.' *OTT! Stop!*

The girls were all looking at her goggle-eyed.

'Marcus did *all* that?' Kendra said.

'Gosh, and here I was thinking Tristan had topped everyone else by his sky writing proposal,' Harriet said with a glum look as she reached for another cupcake.

'Marcus is very romantic when you get to know him,' Juliet said.

'Show us the photos.' Kendra leaned forward expectantly.

Juliet gulped. 'Photos?'

'Yeah, surely you took heaps,' Harriet said, licking

icing off one of her fingers. 'I would've taken more of Tristan's proposal if it hadn't started to rain.'

'I downloaded them off my phone,' Juliet said. 'Sorry.'

Kendra crossed her impossibly skinny legs and picked up her glass again. 'Get Marcus to AirDrop some of his to your phone. He would've taken some surely?'

Juliet swallowed. 'Right… Good idea… I'll do that…'

CHAPTER FIVE

MARCUS HAD SHOWERED and shaved and was sitting in front of his laptop when Juliet came back to the suite. She opened the door tentatively, her gaze averted as if she was worried he might be sitting there stark naked. Her cheeks were bright red and so was the tip of her nose. How many drinks had her friends plied her with? He didn't trust Kendra or her sneaky little sidekick Harriet. He had a feeling they only included Juliet in their group because her more generous figure and understated beauty made them look all the more model-thin and stop-the-traffic gorgeous.

'Sorry.' She tiptoed into the room as if she were crossing a carpet of eggshells. 'I hope I'm not disturbing you.'

Everything about her disturbed him. The way she had felt when he put his arm around her. The way she smelt so homey and yet exotic. The way her freckles made her look so young and innocent. The way her shiny brown hair had natural streaks of mahogany that showed up in the sunshine or under strong lighting. How her figure was not stick thin but curvy and womanly. Her breasts creamy and full, the cleavage deep and tantalising at the neck of her dress. His insides stretched and then coiled tight with lust. She was so sexy but totally unaware of it, which somehow made her even more attractive. 'How'd the tea party go?'

'It was…fun…'

'No male strippers?'

Her cheeks went a shade darker. 'I think there might be one planned for tomorrow night.'

Marcus pushed back his chair and stood. 'I had a call from Ben.'

She put her purse on the coffee table before tucking a strand of hair behind one of her ears. 'I got a call from Mum when I came up in the lift just now.'

'What did you tell her?'

Her gaze was still intent on avoiding his. 'The truth.'

'Always a good idea.'

Her eyes slowly crept up to his, luminous and toffee-brown and as big as Bambi's. 'Marcus?'

'What?'

She rolled her lips together for a moment, her hands tying knots with each other in front of her stomach. 'If you were going to propose to someone…how would you do it?'

Marcus gave an uncomfortable laugh. 'What sort of question is that?'

'It's just—' Her teeth sank into the pillow of her lip. 'I kind of told the girls how you proposed and—'

'*You told them how I proposed?*'

She gave him an exasperated look. 'I had to tell them something. I'm wearing your ring.'

He strode back to his desk and closed the lid of his laptop with a snap. 'It's not *my* ring. It's not even a real diamond.'

'You can *tell* that?'

He looked at her shocked expression. Her eyes were wide and her lush rosy red mouth open in an *O*. Did it really worry her *that* much? Was losing face in front of those vacuous girls *that* important to her? 'I designed a yacht for a diamond dealer a couple of years ago,' he said. 'I can spot a fake a mile off.'

She looked down at her left hand, tilting it from side to side as if to see if it caught the light. 'Do you think the girls will be able to tell? They didn't say anything at tea....'

Marcus shrugged. 'Who knows?'

Her forehead was pleated with worry. 'I couldn't afford to buy a real one. I had to do something quickly. I didn't want them to think you were too tight with money to get me a ring.'

He frowned at her. 'Why would you care what they think about me?'

Her eyes moved away from his. 'I told them you proposed to me on a yacht you designed for a client. I told them it was really romantic with candles and fairy lights and a gourmet picnic and a string quartet playing on deck.'

He coughed out a snort of disdain. 'For God's sake, Juliet, I would *never* propose like that. You're making me sound like a soppy fool.'

'I had to make something up on the spot,' she said.

'If we'd talked about it first we could've got our story organised a bit better. Now they want to see the photos.'

'Photos?'

She gave him another one of her wincing looks. 'I don't suppose you have any photos on your phone of one of your yachts?'

'Plenty,' Marcus said. 'But sadly, not with fairy lights and candles and a string quartet.'

She tugged at her lower lip with her teeth again. 'If you let me have a photo of your most luxurious one I can tell them you were so overwrought with nerves you forgot to take any after you'd decorated it with the lights and stuff. That could work.'

Marcus took out his phone, questioning his sanity as he selected a photo of a yacht he'd designed for a merchant banker last year. 'Will this do?' he asked.

She glanced at the photo, standing so close to him he could smell the flower-fresh scent of her hair. 'That's perfect!' She glanced up at him animatedly. 'It's on the Thames, too.'

He messaged the photo to her before putting his phone back next to his wallet beside his laptop. 'I hate those over-the-top proposals everyone's doing these days,' he said. 'It's such a waste of money. Not only that, it puts pressure on the woman to say yes. If half a million pounds has been spent on setting the scene, how could any woman say no?'

Her gaze was suddenly direct. Confident. Assured. Strident. 'I would say no if I didn't love him. It wouldn't matter how much money he spent.'

'You sure about that, sweet little Juliet?'

Her chin came up a fraction. 'I wouldn't promise to marry anyone I didn't love.'

Marcus studied her expression for a long moment. She was so darned cute when she took a stand. But how would she recognise real love when she was so inexperienced? She was a babe in the woods compared to her snooty-nosed, street-smart friends. He knew she only stayed connected with them because she didn't want to hurt their feelings. How would she protect herself from being exploited by some suave, smooth-talking guy who would sweep her off her feet with candles and fairy lights and string quartets?

She wouldn't stand a chance.

'Ben's worried you'll get taken in by some guy who only wants you for your connection with him.'

Her brown gaze narrowed and sharpened. 'Oh, so I suppose you and he think I can't attract a man in my own right?'

'I didn't say that.'

She stalked to the other side of the room, her arms going across her midsection. 'Just because I'm not a size zero doesn't mean I can't find a man. If I wanted to I could go right out there now and hook up with someone.'

'Not while you're wearing my ring, you won't.'

She swivelled back to look at him archly. 'It's not *your* ring, remember?'

Marcus scooped up his wallet and phone off the writing desk. 'No, but it soon will be.'

Juliet looked at the tray of designer rings the jeweller set before her in a private consulting room a short time later. Glittering diamonds, huge solitaires or princess cut or mosaic settings, others set with blood-red rubies or midnight blue sapphires or creamy pearls. They were all laid out before her in glorious, decadent array. There were no price tags, which meant they were shockingly expensive.

'I'll leave you to discuss your choice in private,' the jeweller said. 'Just press that button there on the wall when you've made your decision.'

Juliet looked at Marcus once the jeweller had closed the door on his exit. 'This is ridiculous. I can't wear a ring that costs more than a house! What if I lose it?'

'I'll insure it.'

She looked at the beautiful mosaic-setting ring that was outshining all the others. It was the most gorgeous ring she had ever seen. From a distance it looked like any other good quality diamond but it was so complicated and intricate when you looked closer. 'I suppose you can always give it back when we've finished using it…'

He picked up the ring she was eyeing and slid it on her finger. 'Looks good. It suits your hand.'

Juliet met his inscrutable gaze. His hand was still holding hers, his fingers warm and strong and protective. Possessive. Something swooped and then dropped in her stomach as he slowly drew her to her feet until she was standing less than half a step from him. Her legs felt strangely unsteady, her breathing patchy, her heart skipping a beat as she felt the magnetic pull of his tall, strong presence drawing her inexorably closer.

She could smell the clean, cologne-fresh scent of

him. She could see the pinpoints of his dark stubble even though he had recently shaved. She could feel the warmth of his body, the intimate closeness of him tempting her beyond her power to resist. His muscled thighs were a mere centimetre or two from hers. Her breasts were even closer to his chest, intensifying the erotic moment. If she leaned forward a few millimetres her nipples would brush against the finely woven cotton of his shirt.

Her awareness of him grew from deep inside her body, stirring all of her dormant senses into zinging wakefulness. Her inner core flickered with a pulse of sudden insistent need. It travelled through her, making her aware of every part of her body, all the sensitive spots and erogenous zones that secretly longed for his touches and caresses.

Did he know how much she wanted him? Could he read it in her face? In her eyes? In her body? Could she feel it in the electrically charged atmosphere?

His dark blue eyes were heavy lidded as they focussed on her mouth for an infinitesimal pause. She couldn't look away if she tried. She was transfixed by the way he was poised there, as if drawing out the anticipation for as long as he could. She took another scatty little breath as his mouth came down ever so slowly towards hers....

Nerves suddenly got the better of her. She hadn't brushed her teeth. What if she reeked of champagne and caramel-swirl cupcakes? She wanted their first kiss to be wonderful, truly memorable. She had dreamed of it since Christmas. How could it happen now when she wasn't even prepared? 'A-aren't we supposed to press the button now?' she said.

'Later,' he said, and sliding his hands up to cup both her cheeks, he covered her mouth with his.

CHAPTER SIX

MARCUS CLOSED HIS eyes as he touched down on the pillow softness of Juliet's mouth. She tasted of sugar and spice and champagne, a heady cocktail unlike any he had tasted before. He pressed gently against the lush fullness of her lips, breathing in the bewitching scent of her, relishing the sweet softness of her mouth as it responded to his. Her lips were slightly parted and he took full advantage of it. He entered her mouth with a smooth glide of his tongue, slowly at first, letting her taste him, feel him. Her tongue was tentative, shy, holding back from him until he deepened the kiss. Then she found her rhythm and joined in the duel with gusto.

Her arms looped around his neck as she stood up on tiptoe, pressing her gorgeous breasts right into his chest. He swore he could feel her nipples poking into his pectoral muscles. How he wanted to feel them in his hands, to touch and caress and taste them, to see if they were as soft and delicious as they looked behind her clothes.

Her pelvis moved against his in an instinctive way, there was nothing forward or brazen about it. She melded against him perfectly, all of her curves fitting against all of his planes. His body responded to her closeness with a painful throb of primal need. Her soft little murmurs of approval as he kept playing with her tongue made his need all the more fervent. Uncontrollable. It pulsed through his body like a raging tide, pounding through his veins, swelling him, extending him until he was as trigger-happy as a teenager on his first date.

He slid one of his hands around the nape of her neck, the cloud of her curly hair bouncing against the back of his hand like sprigs of fragrant summer jasmine. Her sweetness was intoxicating. He couldn't get enough of her. He wanted to devour her right here and now…except they were standing in a room with a CCTV camera documenting every movement they made to the manager and staff in the showroom outside.

Marcus eased back from her, more than a little shocked at how difficult it was to actually do so. He didn't like to think of himself having so little control over his impulses. Especially when he had the rest of the weekend to get through. How was he going to share that bed with her in the privacy of the suite if he couldn't keep his hands off her when they had an audience? 'So, you've decided on the mosaic one, then?' he said with a lightness of tone he was nowhere near feeling.

Her cheeks were a faint pink, her mouth swollen from his kiss and the tiny circle of her chin rosy red from where his stubble had grazed her. It made something inside his stomach slip. 'Are you sure it's not too expensive?' she said.

He reached for the button on the wall. 'Can't have your friends thinking I'm a miser, can we?'

They left the jeweller's soon after and walked back to the hotel. Marcus continued to hold Juliet's hand even though there were no paparazzi outside the front of the hotel; evidently Lucca Chatsfield and his harem of girls had drawn them to a rear exit.

It somehow felt natural to be walking along hand in hand with Marcus. His impressive height made Juliet feel feminine and tiny in comparison. Every now and again his shoulder would brush hers as they navigated their way through the knots of people bustling along the pavement. It sent a shockwave of delight right through her body, making her wonder what it would feel like to be wrapped in his arms, with nothing between them except their skin.

She couldn't get her mind off their kiss, couldn't stop reliving it. The way his lips had felt, the way his tongue had played with hers in such a tantalising fashion. His hands had cupped her face in such a gentle way and yet the explosive power of his mouth had sent an earthquake through her senses. Her feelings for him ballooned inside her until she could think of nothing but how it would feel to make love with him, to be possessed by him…preferably without anyone watching.

'About what happened back there…' Marcus said as they entered the suite back at the hotel.

Juliet knew what was coming. It was the 'It's not

you, it's me' speech she had heard from every guy she had dated in the past. Not that there were many. She hadn't had much luck on the dating scene. She found it hard to be comfortable with men she didn't know well. She knew it was old fashioned and a little out of step with modern dating mores, but she couldn't help it. She was the way she was. She was a hopeless romantic like her father and her mother. 'It was just a kiss, Marcus,' she said airily. 'No big deal.'

He was looking at her with a frown between his brows. 'You know I would never do anything to compromise my friendship with your brother, don't you?'

Pity, Juliet thought. What had her brother got to do with it? If they were attracted to each other why couldn't they leave Ben out of it? But Marcus was a man of honour. He didn't do rash, impulsive things. He went about his life in a careful and considerate manner because his experiences as a child were so chaotic. He liked order and routine because he could control his life better that way.

Hadn't she done the same? Living a quiet life in Bath, spending her days with dust jackets and dust mites. Living in the past because she was too frightened of the future. That's why being part of Kendra's Clan had always been so important, to prove she had what it took to be a modern girl. But did she really have what it took? Why wasn't it feeling as good as she hoped it would?

Juliet moved across the room to put her purse on the coffee table. 'What plans have you got for this evening?'

'Work.'

She turned and looked at him. He was wincing as he rubbed the back of his neck as if his muscles were causing him pain. Guilt assailed her. She had caused him so much bother. He was tired and travel-weary and under work stress, and she had thrown him into a crazy sideshow. How he would hate every minute of pretending to be something he was not. He hated falsity. He hated pretence. He hated shallowness. He had an important meeting on Monday and she had thrown him a curve ball. She had jeopardised everything for him. If he lost the Chatsfield project it would be *all her fault*. 'I'm sorry.'

He dropped his hand and met her gaze. 'For?'

'For ruining your weekend,' she said. 'You've a right to be cross with me. You've worked so hard to get here for the meeting, never once dreaming you would get a walk-on part in a farce of my making. For all I know you might have had plans for a romantic weekend with someone special and I've stuffed it all up. Majorly. Probably permanently now it's all over social media.'

'I wasn't meeting anyone.'

'Not only that, I've made you buy a hideously expensive ring you probably won't be able to take back and get a refund now it's been used.' Juliet grabbed at the sides of her head in frustration. 'Argh! Why do I get myself in these situations? I can't seem to get anything right. How can I be so dumb? Why did I have to *pretend* I had a boyfriend? I mean, who is going to believe it? *Seriously?* I'm too fat and stupid. Who would want me?'

'Lots of guys want you.'

'Name one.'

The silence stretched for a beat or two.

'I want you.'

Juliet swallowed. Did he mean it? Of course he didn't. How could he? That was her dream. It wasn't reality. 'You're just saying that. You feel sorry for me. I know you do. You pity me. You probably talk about me with Ben. *"Poor old Jules, hasn't had a boyfriend since Simon Foster cheated on her with that skinny blonde, how many years ago was it now? Four? Five?"* Go on, admit it, that's what you say, isn't it?'

He came over to her and took her by the shoulders, his fingers warm and strong as they came in contact with her flesh. His sapphire-blue eyes held hers in a mesmerising lock; his body was so close and tempting she could feel her own reacting in little shivers and quivers as each sensually charged second passed. 'I've wanted you for a long time. I haven't acted on it because—' he stroked the pad of his thumb over her bottom lip '—I didn't want to ruin our friendship.'

Juliet's lip buzzed as his thumb passed over it again. 'Why does it have to ruin our friendship?'

He looked at her mouth for a long moment. 'I'm not planning to settle down anytime soon, if ever.'

She tried to quash the pang of disappointment that besieged her. 'Just because your parents were unhappy doesn't mean you will be.'

He gave her a rueful twist of a smile and dropped his hands from her shoulders. She could tell he had made up his mind. A shutter had come down. The decision had been made. He wouldn't go back on it. 'You want the husband and the house and the hound by the fireside. I'm not that guy to give you that. Sorry.'

Juliet watched in dismay as he moved across to his laptop. He was focussed on work now. Not on her. She had been rejected years ago for a size-zero blonde and now she was being rejected for a laptop.

Story of her life.

Marcus pretended to be engrossed in the PowerPoint presentation he had prepared on his laptop when Juliet came out of the bathroom dressed for the nightclub party. She was wearing a black cocktail dress with a scooped neckline that showcased her breasts rather spectacularly. She had on sky-high heels and her shiny brown hair was swirled up on top of her head in an artfully arranged style that somehow looked casual and elegant at the same time. Her eye makeup highlighted the depth and shape of her brown eyes and the mascara she was wearing made her eyelashes look like miniature black fans. Her lips were full and glossy with a shimmering lip gloss, and she smelt of summer flowers with an understory of musk that sent his senses into a tailspin. How he had kept himself from proving how much he wanted her earlier was still a mystery to him. It had been touch-and-go. He could still feel the throb of longing in his body.

It didn't matter if she was dressed up or dressed down, make-up on or make-up off, hair loose or tied up. He wanted her.

How could he endure this torture? He had two nights

to get through with her in the bed beside him. It was bad enough listening to her having a shower. His mind was still filled with images of her luscious body all wet and soapy and slippery. His fingers had itched to open the door and join her, to slide his hands over her delicious curves, to bury himself deep inside her.

'Don't wait up,' she said.

Marcus clicked on the next slide. 'What time will you be back?' *Sheesh, you sound like her guardian.*

'Not sure.' She fiddled with her droplet earring. 'I'll see how it goes. I might get lucky. Who knows?'

Marcus swivelled on his chair to look at her front on. His frown was so intense he could feel his eyebrows touching. 'You're supposed to be engaged. That means you don't flirt with other guys. You don't accept drinks from other guys and you sure as hell don't go back to their room. Okay?'

She gave him a pert look. 'Who's going to stop me?'

Who *was* going to stop her? She had a perfect right to go out and have a good time. She was young and single. She was gorgeous and sweet. Some other guy would snap her up in a heartbeat. It wasn't as if *he* was offering her anything...*was he?*

He worked his jaw. 'Look, I know you're a little angry with me about not taking things further but—'

'It's fine, Marcus. Really.' She picked up her evening purse, popped a wand of lip gloss inside it and snapped it closed. She gave him a bright smile. 'How do I look?'

Ravishing. Sexy. Irresistible. 'Can you walk in those heels?'

'Not really, but then I can hardly breathe in this

dress.' She smoothed her hands down over her hips, a little frown pulling at her forehead. 'I wonder if I should've got the bigger size?'

Marcus had to work hard to keep his eyes above her neckline. 'You look great.'

'It's not designer or anything,' she went on as if he hadn't spoken. 'That's why I cut the label out. Besides, I don't want Harriet peeking at what size it is and posting it on Facebook or Twitter.'

'Why do you let her get to you?'

Her teeth pulled at her lower lip. 'I don't know what you mean....'

'Yes, you do. You let her bully you. You've let her put you down since you were a teenager. Why don't you stand up to her? To all of them?'

Her eyes moved away from his. 'I have to get going. I don't want to be late.'

'They're not your friends, Juliet,' Marcus said as she opened the door to leave.

She sent him a frosty look. 'So, you and Ben think I can't get a man *and* I can't attract genuine friends. Thanks a bunch. Love the confidence you guys have in me.'

Marcus winced as the door clicked shut. 'Nice job, Bainbridge.'

CHAPTER SEVEN

JULIET WAS DETERMINED not to be the first to leave the nightclub party. She danced with the girls until her feet were aching and her ears were ringing from the loud music. She was having fun. Of course she was. She was out partying with her friends. Marcus could think what he liked.

Kendra came over with a cocktail in one hand and party streamers in the other. 'Have you seen Harriet?' she asked.

Juliet scanned the dance floor. It was a pulsating mass of scantily clad female bodies with some impressive male ones doing all sorts of gyrations she thought were anatomically impossible. 'Not recently. She might have gone to the ladies' room. Do you want me to find her for you?'

'No, that's okay.' Kendra sat on the leather love seat beside her and eased her feet out of her stilettoes. 'God, my feet are killing me.'

'Same.'

Kendra wriggled her neatly manicured toes. 'Can I ask you something?'

Juliet glanced at her but she was still looking at her feet. 'Sure.'

The leather squeaked as Kendra turned to look at her. 'How did you know Marcus was The One?'

Juliet had no trouble thinking of an answer. It was just there. In her head. In her heart. How had she not realised it until now? 'I just knew. I think maybe I've always known on some subconscious level. But the first time he kissed me sealed it.'

Kendra's smile had a touch of wistfulness about it. 'You're lucky.... To be so certain, I mean.'

Juliet looked at her with a frown. 'And you're not? About Hugh?'

Kendra let out a sigh and directed her gaze back to her feet. 'I don't know.... It felt so right when he proposed. But now with the wedding just a week away I'm not so sure.'

'Maybe it's just wedding jitters.'

'Maybe.'

A silence slipped past...not that it was really a silence given the loud music thumping in the background.

Juliet wondered what had brought on Kendra's uncertainty. She was normally such a confident, outgoing type. Juliet had always envied Kendra's self-possession and poise. Kendra had been Head Girl at school. She was Head Girl wherever she went. She was rich and beautiful and popular. She had a fiancé who loved her. *A real fiancé.* Hugh Pritchard was gorgeous and successful and had dated Kendra for three and a half years. He wasn't a phantom fiancé who would disappear on Monday morning.

'I wish I hadn't asked Harriet to be my maid of honour,' Kendra said.

Juliet wondered if it was the alcohol talking. Kendra had been knocking back the cocktails with gay abandon and Juliet hadn't seen her eat a thing all evening. 'What makes you say that?'

She lifted one of her thin, spray-tanned shoulders in a little shrug. 'I don't know…I guess I thought she'd do a good job.'

'She *is* doing a good job.'

'I know but it's not like I'm close to her. I mean *really* close.'

'I thought you were best friends?'

Kendra turned the engagement ring on her finger a couple of times. 'She's so…out there, you know? It gets a little wearing after a while.' She stopped twirling and looked at Juliet with a wry smile. 'Maybe I've finally grown up.'

Juliet smiled back. 'Maybe we all have.'

Marcus was sitting in the bar area taking a long time to drink a brandy and dry when he saw Juliet come out of the nightclub. He convinced himself he'd only come down to check she didn't leave with some totally unsuitable guy. But the truth was he was here because he wanted to be with her himself. How could he not want her? How had he resisted her for so long? Where were his reason and logic now? His impulses were in the driver's seat and they had their foot to the floor. He didn't want her hooking up with some stranger. If she wanted to hook up with someone, she could hook up with him.

Her evening purse was swinging from its chain where it was curled around one of her fingers. Her hair was more down than up, her lip gloss had worn off, and it looked like she was limping, but he had never seen her look more beautiful.

He left his drink on the bar to intercept her. 'Hey.'

She blinked and then smiled but it didn't quite reach her eyes. 'I'm only talking to you because we're supposed to be engaged.'

'I guess there's logic in that statement somewhere.'

She flashed him a narrowed look. 'Are you checking up on me?'

'Do I need to?'

She let out a sigh that made her shoulders drop. 'No, of course not. I was coming up to bed—' Her cheeks went bright red. 'I mean up to the room.'

'Fancy a drink first?'

Her brow puckered. 'A…a drink?'

He kept his expression poker-faced. 'It doesn't have to be alcohol. We can have a hot chocolate if you prefer.'

She scowled at him from beneath her lashes. 'I'm not twelve.'

He stroked her pink cheek with his fingertip. 'Don't be mad at me.'

He felt her quiver under his touch, her brown eyes softening, and her pursed lips relaxing. 'One drink, okay?'

'And a dance?'

Her eyes rounded. 'You want to…to dance?'

Marcus took her by the hand. 'Are your feet up to it?'

'I'll take my shoes off.'

'Just your shoes?'

She angled her head at him, a tiny glint sparkling in her eyes. 'Are you flirting with me, Marcus?'

He brought her up close and then lowered his mouth to hers. 'I haven't even started.'

Juliet couldn't recall later how they got to the suite. It seemed one minute they were kissing in the middle of the bar area and the next they were in the privacy of their hotel room. All she could remember of the trip up in the elevator was the thrill of Marcus's mouth fused to hers. She was dazed by his desire for her. She could feel the hardened heat of him as he crushed her mouth beneath his as he walked her into the suite. It was as if her entire life she had been waiting for this moment. For the moment when he would take her in his arms and claim her. To own his need of her.

'I want you naked,' he said against her mouth, his hand warm and firm on her hips.

'I thought you didn't want to—'

'I want to.' He kissed the side of her neck. 'I want to so badly.'

'I'm going to need some help with this zip.' She turned and lifted her hair out of the way, shivering when his hands slid the zipper down to the dip in her spine.

He kept her there in front of him, his mouth blazing a hot trail against the sensitive skin of her neck. 'Do you have any idea of how long I've wanted to do this?' He unclipped her bra and slid his hands around to cup her breasts. The feel of his hands touching her so intimately made her shudder with pleasure. His thumbs found her nipples, rolling over them in tantalising movements that made her toes curl into the soft carpet. She could feel his erection against the cheeks of her bottom, a spine-tingling reminder of the erotic power they were about to unleash.

He spun her around and looked at her with hungry eyes, feasting on her, taking in her naked breasts and the curve of her belly. She had never felt more desirable. More beautiful. He made her feel like a goddess by the way he was touching her with his gaze, heating her flesh to boiling point. 'You're so gorgeous.' He circled her nipples in turn, making her shiver in delight.

Juliet set to work on his shirt buttons but her fingers were as good as useless. In the end he whipped it off over his head and tossed it to the floor. She undid his belt and trouser fastening and he stepped out of them as she shimmied out of her dress.

He searched her gaze for a beat. 'Are you sure about this?'

She slipped her hand beneath his undershorts, discovering him, caressing him. Wanting him. 'Never surer.'

He crushed her mouth to his as his hands went back to her hips, holding her against him as his tongue tangoed with hers in a sultry dance of lust and long-denied cravings. Her body was so ready for him. She could feel the dew of her arousal between her thighs, could feel the racing of her heart as his mouth continued to wreak sensual havoc on hers.

His hands moved from her hips to her bottom, pulling her close to his hard heat, enticing her with the force and power of his need. 'God, this is madness but I can't stop.'

'I don't want you to stop.' She nipped at his lower lip, pulling at it with her teeth in a playful bite. 'I want you to make love to me all night long.'

He shuddered as she took him in her hands again. 'I'm supposed to be working.'

She stroked her tongue over his top lip. 'You have plenty of time tomorrow. The meeting's not till Monday.'

He nudged and nipped at her lower lip, his brandy-scented breath mingling with hers. 'I don't trust Gene Chatsfield or his ruthless new CEO. One or both of them could easily bring the meeting forward.'

Juliet eased back to look at him. 'Why would they do that?'

He trailed a scorching pathway of kisses from her earlobe to the corner of her mouth. 'As a test.' He pressed a hot kiss to her lips. 'To see which of the three of us is the best prepared.'

She shivered as his lips moved back to her earlobe. 'But doesn't it depend on who has the best design?'

'It should but it doesn't always. Business can be cut-throat. The best man doesn't always win.'

Juliet stroked his lean jaw as she gazed into his eyes. 'I want you to win.'

His eyes were inky-dark and determined. 'That's the plan.'

She closed her eyes as his mouth came back down, sweeping her into a maelstrom of sensation. She felt the swell of desire move through her body, rolling over her in waves with each stroke and glide of his tongue.

He pulled her knickers down and she stepped out of them, snatching in a breath and holding it as his gaze slowly moved over her. 'So beautiful…' His voice was deep and gravelly, his touch like fire as he traced the seam of her body.

She leaned into his touch, instinctively searching for the release she craved. She gasped as he entered her with one of his fingers, the slippery glide of it making her body pulsate with pleasurable shockwaves. 'I want you,' she whispered against his mouth. 'All of you.'

He led her to the huge bed, stripping back the covers with a quick movement of his hand that made a rush of excitement storm through her body. He stepped out of his underwear before he joined her. His legs were hairy and rough against hers, his body hard against her softness. But instead of feeling self-conscious about her body, she felt proud. He gave her no other choice. She could tell he was delighted in her every curve because of the way he kissed and caressed each one. Her breasts, her stomach, her thighs were all worshipped by his lips and tongue.

Juliet clutched at the sheet when he brought his mouth to the juncture of her thighs. He must have sensed her hesitancy as he placed a gentle hand on her belly. 'Relax, I won't rush you.'

She closed her eyes and let the sensations wash over her as he caressed her. Each stroke of his tongue brought her closer to the summit. She could feel it building like a storm cloud about to burst. It swelled and swelled until finally it broke free with an earth-shattering explosion that fanned out from her core to every pore of her body.

He moved up her body, kissing her skin all the way, lingering over her breasts until her nipples were red and glistening with his warm saliva. 'You have the most amazing breasts.'

Juliet stroked him with her fingers. 'You have the most amazing body.'

His eyes smouldered. 'Now might be a good time for a condom.'

'You have one?'

'In my wallet.' He left her on the bed while he went in search of his wallet. She drank in the sight of him, so lean and strong and powerfully irresistibly male.

'How many do you have?'

'Three.'

She arched an eyebrow. 'Only three?'

His look melted her bones. 'It's a start. I can get more tomorrow.' He tore the edge of the condom seal with his teeth. Juliet watched as he rolled the condom over his erection, her body singing in anticipation as he came back to join her on the bed. He positioned himself between her thighs, one of his legs hitched up so she didn't have to take his full weight. He kissed her long and deep, ramping up her need all over again. Her body hungered for him, her insides twisting and turning and tightening with longing until she was whimpering beneath the pressure of his mouth.

He gently parted her to receive him, slowly entering her so she could gradually accommodate him. Her body wrapped around him, gripping him tightly as he began to thrust. She heard him draw in a quick breath as if her body had surprised him. Delighted him. 'You feel so good,' he groaned against her lips.

She quivered all over as he upped his pace. It was as if his body had set its own rhythm in response to hers. His thrusts became deeper and harder and faster, his breathing as hectic and breathless as her own. Sensations showered through her flesh like a fountain of bubbles moving through her blood. The tension gathered in her pelvis, the swollen bud of her arousal silently begging for the friction it needed. She lifted her hips at the same time as he brought his hand between their rocking bodies. It was all she needed to fly. She came with a rush that shook her body in giant spasms of delight, each one like a wave cresting through her.

His release followed on the tail end of hers. She felt each erotic shudder, heard his guttural groan as he emptied. She held him to her, reluctant to break the connection before all the sensations had subsided. His head was buried beside her neck, his warm breath caressing her skin, his chest rising and falling on hers.

He finally eased back on his elbows to look down at her. 'No regrets?'

Juliet touched her fingertips to the sculptured perfection of his mouth. 'None whatsoever. You?'

He nibbled at her fingers, his eyes holding hers. 'So, you want the left side of the bed, right?'

She smiled as she traced a line down the length of his nose. 'Am I going to have to wrestle with you for it?'

He gave her a wickedly sexy grin that made her spine loosen. 'What do you think?'

CHAPTER EIGHT

JULIET HAD BEEN awake for an hour, watching Marcus sleep beside her, when he suddenly jolted upright with a short, sharp expletive. He threw off the covers and leapt out of bed. 'What time is it? What day is it?'

'It's seven-thirty on Saturday.'

He rubbed a hand down his face. 'I had a dream. A nightmare.'

She sat up and hugged the sheet around her knees. 'What was it about?'

He raked a hand through his sleep tousled jet-black hair. 'I dreamed I missed the meeting. I got the day wrong. I turned up on the wrong day.' He shook his head and gave a relieved sounding laugh. 'It was just a dream.'

Juliet rested her chin on the top of her knees. 'Why is this project so important to you? It's not as though it's the biggest project you've done. Surely the sheikh's was bigger?'

He sat on the edge of the bed next to her. 'It's not the size of the project.' He trailed a fingertip down her arm from her shoulder to her wrist, making her skin lift in a shiver of reaction. 'You know that Biblical saying about a prophet not being welcome in their own country?'

Juliet looked into his dark blue eyes; she saw the determination there, the drive and steely ambition. He was so centred and focussed. Goal-oriented. She had always admired that about him. He worked hard and didn't allow anything to distract him from his mission. 'You want this more than anything, don't you?'

He took her hand and turned it over in his, stroking her palm with the broad pad of his thumb in a slow caress that triggered a hot spurt of longing deep in her pelvis. 'The Chatsfields are one of Britain's richest families. To design a yacht for them would open lots of doors for me here and abroad.'

Juliet touched his stubbly face with her hand. 'Why do you push yourself so hard?'

He held her hand to his face by covering it with his own. 'You already know the answer to that.'

'Because you don't want to be labelled a layabout aristocrat like your father.'

He gave her a wry smile. 'There you go. A direct quote from one of the tabloids.'

She studied his expression for a moment. 'Where do you go after here? Back to Dubai?'

He stood and ploughed his hand back through his hair. 'Let's not have this conversation right now, okay?'

Juliet pinched her lips together. *Fool. Why did you spoil it all?* 'I'm sorry.'

He let out a harsh sounding breath. 'I knew this would be a mistake. Sex blurs the boundaries too much. I wish I'd never—'

'Don't say it.' She stared at her knees. 'No regrets, okay? This is just for the weekend. I know that. I'm okay with that.' *No, I'm not!*

He came back over to the bed, sat beside her and turned her face towards him with the tip of his finger beneath her chin. 'Are you sure?'

Juliet ignored the tight spasm of pain in her chest. His eyes were so dark they reminded her of deep outer space—infinite and unreachable. 'It's my fault we're in this situation and I accept full responsibility for it, but don't worry, it will be over soon.'

It was his turn to study her expression for a beat. 'Why is it so important to you to keep up the pretence? Why couldn't you just tell them the truth?'

Juliet rolled her eyes as she shoved his hand away to get off the bed. 'Oh yeah, why didn't *I* think of that?' She whipped a bathrobe off a hook next to the wardrobe and pushed her arms through the sleeves. 'I could tell them I haven't had a date in five years because I got screwed around by a two-timing jerk and I lost my confidence because he said I was fat and ugly to one of his friends who posted it online. I could tell them I'm terrified because I'm twenty-nine next month and I'm worried I'm never going to find someone who loves me enough to marry me and have a family with me. I could tell them all my fears and have them look at me pityingly, or worse, have them set me up on horrid blind dates. I won't do it, Marcus. And you can't make me.'

The silence was deafening. Shaming. Embarrass-ing. Excruciating.

He took a step towards her but she held up her hand. 'No. Please. Don't make this any worse.'

'Juliet...I—'

'I know what you're going to say.' She met his gaze head-on. 'You're going to say "it's not you, it's me," right?'

His eyes looked pained. 'This is all I can give you right now. I'm sorry.'

Juliet gave him a cynical look before she turned for the bathroom. 'It's just another version of the same thing, isn't it?'

Marcus wasn't in the suite when Juliet came out of the bathroom. She was relieved and disappointed. Relieved she didn't have to see him feeling sorry for her now she'd laid all her secrets bare. Disappointed he wasn't there to tell her he loved her and wanted her to spend the rest of her life with him. She knew it was foolish to dream. Foolish to hope. Foolish to fall in love with someone who was so far out of her reach.

But she had *always* loved him. She couldn't remember a time when she hadn't. As a child she had loved him as a brother, and then, as she got older, as a friend. But now she loved him as lover. A life partner, except he didn't want her for life. Just for a measly weekend.

The girls were waiting for her in the Chatsfield spa for their day of pampering. Juliet pasted on a smile and joined in with the luxurious treatments, listening to the chatter and gossip with one ear while her mind drifted elsewhere.

But that just about summed it up.

She was always on the outer edge. Looking in instead of at the centre. She was a fringe person. No one noticed her sitting on the sidelines.

Story of her life.

Harriet came over with a glass of champagne with a strawberry perched on the rim of the glass. 'There's been a change of plans for this evening.'

'Oh?'

'I know it's a break with hen's weekend protocol but since Hugh and Tristan are in town for an investment conference, and you've got Marcus here, we thought we'd have a couples' dinner tonight. Just the six of us.'

'Dinner?' Juliet looked at her in alarm. 'What happened to the male stripper?'

'Kendra was having qualms about it. Said she didn't want you to feel uncomfortable.' Harriet sat on the arm of the leather pedicure chair opposite Juliet's. 'It will be a good chance for Marcus to meet the boys. Will he be free?'

Juliet swallowed. 'I'll have to check…'

Harriet's smile was as sly as a fox sizing up an unsuspecting chicken. 'He surely won't be too busy for his fiancée, will he?'

Marcus was coming back from the hotel gym where he had worked off some, but not all, of his unsettled feelings. He had run twelve kilometres on the treadmill. Pushed a few weights around. Done three hundred abdominal crunches, and yet he still couldn't get Juliet's hurt expression out of his mind. It had never been his intention to hurt her. He was annoyed with himself for letting things get out of his control. He'd had this same conversation with himself at Christmas. He'd known it would get messy. Relationships always did, which was why he avoided them. Juliet had always been a part of his life. He didn't want that to change. He couldn't bear for it to change. But he wasn't the answer to her problem.

He wasn't anyone's answer.

A tall, imposing figure came towards him down the corridor. Christos Giantrakos was dressed suavely in a suit and crisp shirt and neatly knotted tie, making Marcus feel at a distinct disadvantage dressed in sweaty gym gear. But maybe that was the point.

Christos offered his hand. 'Marcus Bainbridge, isn't it?'

'Yes. How do you do?'

'I noticed your name on the bookings. Welcome to the Chatsfield.'

There would be little that escaped the sharp-eyed Greek's notice, Marcus thought. 'Thank you.'

Christos glanced at his phone to access his calendar. 'Your appointment with us was scheduled for Monday.'

'That's correct.'

Christos slipped his phone into his pocket and met his gaze directly. Challengingly. 'How do you feel about bringing it forward?'

Juliet was in the suite when Marcus came out of the bathroom after his shower. She was standing across from the bed where he had laid out his suit, shirt and tie in readiness for the pitch meeting. Her cheeks were pink and her teeth were starkly white against her lower lip as she chewed at it. 'Are you going out?'

'I was right about Giantrakos.' He reached for his shirt. 'He brought the meeting forward to tonight. A private dinner in the boardroom with him and Gene Chatsfield.'

'Oh…just as well you're so well prepared.'

Marcus studied her while he buttoned his shirt. Her eyes were averted but whether that was because he was half naked or because she was still upset with him was hard to gather. Her forehead was creased as if she was fretting about something. Was she regretting making love with him? Had he ruined everything between them? Something moved in his chest, like a gear shifting but only halfway. The blocked feeling stole his breath. He needed to talk to her but not like this. Not while his mind was on the meeting.

'What are your plans for this evening?' he asked.

Her eyes kept skittering away from his. 'Just dinner with the girls.'

'Want to meet up afterwards?'

She stretched her mouth into a tight smile. 'It's okay, Marcus. You don't have to babysit me.'

'Can we talk when I get back from the meeting?'

She looked away again. 'I think we've said all that needs to be said.'

Marcus wasn't so sure he had said all he needed to say. The words he wanted to say were still jumbled inside his head. They were all out of order like a puzzle he couldn't quite solve. That ache in his chest wouldn't go away. It was cramped. Tight. Stuck. But then, hadn't it been that way since Christmas? He thought he'd had his life all planned. He didn't have room for feelings that were complicated and confusing. He needed time to process it all. 'This isn't going to ruin our friendship, is it?'

She smiled again but it was brittle around the edges. 'Of course not.'

He came over to her and held her by the shoulders. 'You're a beautiful person, Juliet. You deserve to have it all. Don't let anyone tell you different.'

She slipped from out of his hold. 'I have to get ready for dinner. I'll see you later.'

Marcus was on his way to the boardroom when he ran into Harriet Penhallon. She glanced at his laptop. 'Aren't you joining us for dinner?' she asked.

Something about the way she was eyeing him made him feel uncomfortable. Uneasy. Suspicion began to march with ice-cold feet over his scalp. 'Dinner?'

'Didn't Juliet tell you? We're having a couples' dinner in the restaurant downstairs.' She gave him a glinting smile. 'Only affianced couples are invited.'

A flood of feeling spread through his chest, unblocking the jammed gear like a flow of warmed oil over rust. Juliet hadn't asked him to go with her because she knew how important his meeting was to him. She hadn't even *mentioned* the dinner in case he felt pressured. She had put her needs aside in preference for his.

Who else in his life ever *did* that?

She had decided to go to the dinner alone, facing certain social suicide rather than compromise his work commitments. Why had he doubted his feelings for her? Hadn't he always adored that about her? She was always giving, looking after others, and putting her own needs on hold. It was like a light coming on in his head, illuminating the one emotion he had been spending years assiduously avoiding. Ignoring. Denying.

Love.

His work wasn't the most important thing in his life.

The most important thing in his life—*the most important person in his life*—was Juliet.

'Where's Marcus?' Kendra asked as Juliet came into the restaurant.

'Erm…there's something I need to tell you.'

Kendra looked past her shoulder. 'Oh, *there* he is. Hi, Marcus. I'd like to you meet my fiancé, Hugh.'

Juliet blinked a couple of times to clear her vision in case she was imagining it was Marcus standing there looking tall and debonair as introductions were made. Her heart was jumping around her chest like a mad thing. He was here? What about his meeting? Had it been rescheduled? Postponed? A knife of disappointment slashed her hopes to ribbons. *Duh.* Obviously it had been postponed. Why else would he be here?

He came over and slipped an arm around her shoulders. 'Sorry I'm late, darling.' He pressed a soft kiss to her mouth. 'Were you worried I wouldn't make it?'

Juliet looked into his twinkling dark blue eyes. He was acting for the girls and doing a remarkably convincing job of it. But something about his smile made her heart leap from its moorings.

He *was* acting…*wasn't he?*

'What about your meeting?'

'I cancelled it.'

Shock rendered her speechless for a moment. '*You* cancelled it?'

'Yep.'

'It wasn't Christos or Gene Chatsfield?'

'Nope.'

Her mouth dropped open. 'But…but *why?*'

His midnight-blue eyes danced some more. 'I suddenly realised there were far more important things I had to do.'

She swallowed a lump of emotion that was threatening to choke her. 'You cancelled it…*for me?*'

He took her hands in his and squeezed them tightly. 'Why's that so hard for you to believe? You deserve to be put first.'

Juliet couldn't believe he was standing there holding her as if he never wanted to let her go. 'You don't have to do this, Marcus. I was going to tell the girls the truth.'

He brought her closer, his hands holding both of hers against his thudding heart. 'The truth is I love you. I think I've loved you for as long as I've known you. Like a little sister in the early years and then as a friend. But last Christmas something changed. I backed away from it because it was too…I don't know…I guess because I was worried it would change everything. But it *had* already changed everything, hadn't it? There was no going back.'

Juliet felt hope swell and spread in her chest until

she could scarcely breathe. He *loved* her? 'I feel the same. I can't remember not loving you. I think that's why I haven't dated in so long. I couldn't bear to be with anyone but you.'

His smile made her heart skip again. 'Will you marry me?'

Juliet closed her eyes for a beat. 'Okay, so now I'm going to open my eyes and find this is all a dream.' She opened them again but he was still there. '*Am* I dreaming?'

Marcus laughed. 'I guess I need some fairy lights and candles and a string quartet to convince you. And I should probably call your mother. Your brother as well, which, quite frankly, scares the heck out of me as I'm really quite fond of my kneecaps, but still. A man's gotta do what a man's gotta do.' His eyes glinted again. 'So, what are you doing after dinner? Do you fancy a little sail on the Thames?'

She smiled as his arms came around her. 'I wouldn't miss it for the world.'

* * * * *

*Turn the page for a sneak peek at
Book One of* THE CHATSFIELD

*SHEIKH'S SCANDAL
by
Lucy Monroe*

CHAPTER ONE

NOT EASILY IMPRESSED, Liyah Amari very nearly stopped to gawp upon entering the Chatsfield London for the first time.

Flagship of the Chatsfield family's hotel empire, the lodging preferred by Europe's elite was magnificent.

San Francisco's property where her mother had worked since before Liyah's birth was beautiful, but nothing compared to the opulence of this hotel. From the liveried doormen to the grandeur of the ballroom-size lobby, she felt as if she'd stepped into a bygone era of luxury.

A decidedly frenetic air of anticipation and preparation was at odds with the elegant surroundings, though. One maid rushed through the lobby—which Liyah was certain was anything but a normal occurrence—while another polished the walnut banisters of the grand staircase.

It looked like an impromptu but serious meeting was happening near the concierge desk. The desk reception staff were busy with the phone and computer, respectively, checking in an attractive elderly couple.

"Welcome to the Chatsfield London, Mr. and Mrs. Michaels. Here is your room key," the young man said, "and here is your complimentary hospitality pack. We very much hope that you enjoy your stay."

Both staff were too busy to pay attention to who might be entering the hotel. Behind reception, Liyah saw a row of photographs depicting the Chatsfield London's staff. Something in her chest tightened as she caught the image of Lucilla Chatsfield staring back at her from within a frame.

One of the Chatsfield siblings Liyah admired and wished she could get to know, Lucilla was too far up the hotel's ranks for that to ever be likely.

A noise from behind her dragged her attention to where maintenance was replacing a bulb in the giant chandelier that cast the saffron walls with an elegant glow. Ecru moldings and columns added a tasteful but subtly lavish touch and the faint but lingering smell of fresh paint indicated they'd had a recent tidying up.

Liyah's sensible shoes made no noise as she crossed the black-and-white marble-tiled floor, heading directly for the elevator as she'd been instructed to do.

A man stepped in front of her. "May I help you find someone?"

His tone and expression were polite, but it had to be obvious to him that Liyah in her well-fitting but conservative black gabardine suit was not a guest at the Chatsfield.

"I have an appointment with Mrs. Miller." As was her usual habit, Liyah was fifteen minutes early for her meeting with the senior housekeeper.

The man's eyes lit up. "Oh, you must be the maid from Zeena Sahra."

No. That had been her mother. "I am familiar with Zeena Sahran culture, but I was born in America."

Liyah had been hired as a floor supervising chambermaid on the presidential level with special concierge services, just below the hotel's penthouse suites. With hospitality as well as housekeeping duties, she would be working in tandem with the concierge team in a new initiative designed to increase customer satisfaction.

It would be a much more satisfying job for Liyah than the one her mother had held for almost three decades and Hena would have approved wholeheartedly.

"Yes, of course. The elevator is right this way." The man started walking. "I will have to key your access to the basement level."

"Thank you."

Liyah was still a few minutes early when she knocked on the senior housekeeper's office door.

"Enter," came from within.

Mrs. Miller was a tall, thin woman who wore a more severe version of Liyah's suit with a starched white blouse buttoned all the way up.

"I'm pleased you are here, Miss Amari, but I hope you've come prepared to begin work immediately," she said after the pleasantries were out of the way.

"Yes, of course."

"Good. Your concierge floor has been booked for the sheikh's harem." Mrs. Miller gave a disdainful sniff with the word *harem*.

"Excuse me? A sheikh from Zeena Sahra is coming to stay?" And he needed an *entire floor* for his harem?

No wonder they'd wanted to transfer her mother from the Chatsfield San Francisco.

"Yes, Sheikh bin Falah will be staying with us for two weeks. His fiancée will be joining him for the second one."

Liyah schooled the shock from her features. "Sheikh al Zeena, or Sheikh bin Falah al Zeena, but he would not be referred to as Sheikh bin Falah. To do so would cause offence."

Liyah wasn't sure about correcting her boss, but she assumed this sort of knowledge was why she'd been hired.

At least now she understood the need for her *expertise*. Not just a tribal sheikh but the crown prince of Zeena Sahra was coming to stay at the Chatsfield London.

Probably the single most gorgeous man alive, he could easily be an international playboy with a string of super-models hanging on his arm. However, he had a reputation for being buttoned-down and focused entirely on his duties as emir of Zeena Sahra.

"I see. I'll make a note of it. I presume addressing him as Your Highness is acceptable."

"It is, though from what I have read, since Zeena Sahra is an emirate, he prefers the title of *emir*."

Mrs. Miller's mouth pursed. "Why didn't we know this?"

"It's a small thing, really."

"No," Mrs. Miller said sharply. "There's nothing

small about this visit from the sheikh. Every detail must be seen to with absolute attention. If not, mistakes happen. Only last week someone wanted to send silk napkins to the Chatsfield Preitalle with the inscription 'Princess Maddie.' Can you believe it? For a royal wedding? This is why each detail *must* be perfect."

"I will do my best."

"Yes. In addition to your usual duties, for the duration of the sheikh's visit, you will also personally oversee the housekeeping staff for his suite and the adjoining rooms for his security people."

Nothing like being thrown in at the deep end, but Liyah didn't mind. She thrived on a challenge.

Nevertheless, it was a good thing Liyah had gotten her degree in hospitality management. It didn't hurt either that she'd cleaned rooms at the Chatsfield San Francisco every summer break through high school and college, not that her mother had encouraged Liyah to make her career there.

Quite the opposite, Hena had been adamant that her daughter *not* work for the Chatsfield. And now that she knew what she did, maybe Liyah understood that better.

After a somewhat harried orientation, during which staff members she met asked as many questions of Liyah about Zeena Sahra as she asked them about the Chatsfield London, she returned to her newly rented bedsit.

About the size of a college dorm room with an efficiency kitchen and miniscule bath tacked on, it was a far cry from the two-bedroom apartment with a balcony she'd shared with her mother in San Francisco.

An apartment she'd been only too happy to move out of when she got the floor supervisory position with the Chatsfield London.

The job offer was a brilliant coincidence that Liyah's mother would have called destiny. But then Hena Amari had had a romantic streak her daughter did not share.

Although her outlook on life was decidedly more pragmatic, once Liyah had seen the contents of her mother's safety-deposit box and read Hena's final letter, she'd known she had to come to England.

The new job had allowed her to do so without dipping too deeply into what was left from the proceeds of her mother's life insurance policy. The money had been welcome if entirely unexpected. The policy had been one of the many profound shocks Liyah had found in that safety-deposit box.

Shocks that had ultimately ended with her working for the Chatsfield London.

The hotel had been looking specifically for someone with knowledge of Zeena Sahran culture and hospitality norms. Ironically, they had contacted the San Francisco property's senior housekeeper, Stephanie Carter, in hopes of transferring Hena Amari.

With Hena's sudden death, Stephanie, knowing about Liyah, had suggested her instead. Even though Liyah had not worked for the Chatsfield San Francisco since the summer before her last year of university, her education and experience had made her uniquely eligible for a newly created position.

The irony that a job with the hotel would make it

possible for her daughter to fulfill Hena's final wish was not lost on Liyah.

Liyah did not resent her mother's silence on any front, but only superb emotional control had allowed her to take one stunning revelation after another without cracking.

On the outside.

The most stunning revelation of all had been that the extremely wealthy English hotelier Gene Chatsfield was Liyah's biological father.

After years of seeing the exploits of his legitimate children in the tabloid press, Liyah found it nearly impossible to believe his blood ran through her veins. What did she, a woman who had worked hard for everything she had, have in common with this notorious, spoiled family?

She had an almost morbid curiosity to discover what kind of man raised his children to be so profligate while sending the most meager of stipends to Hena on Liyah's behalf.

The answer might lie in the very fact of Liyah's existence, the result of Gene's indulgence in numerous affairs with his hotel maids. Affairs that did *not* make it into the press.

Hena hadn't known about the hotelier's wife, much less his propensity for seducing the chambermaids, until after he left San Francisco and a pregnant Hena behind. It had all been in the final letter Hena had left Liyah.

She'd never told another soul the identity of Liyah's father. Hena's shame in the fact he'd been a married man colored the rest of her life and yet she'd written in her letter that Liyah needed to forgive him.

Hena had claimed that Gene Chatsfield was not a villain, not a demon, not even a very bad man. But he had been a man going through a very bad time. Her final request had been for Liyah to come to London and make herself known to her father.

Liyah would respect her mother's last wishes, but she was happy to have the opportunity to observe the man incognito—as an employee, not the daughter he'd never acknowledged.

Her uniform crisp, her long black hair caught in an impeccable bun, Liyah stood tucked away in a nook near the grand staircase. She'd been in London two weeks and working at the Chatsfield ten hectic days, but had yet to catch a glimpse of her father.

Word had come down that the Honorable Sheikh Sayed bin Falah al Zeena was arriving today, though. Liyah had no doubts her father would be on hand to greet the sheikh personally.

One thing that had become patently obvious in the past ten days: the sheikh's stay was incredibly important to the hotel, and even more significant to the Chatsfield's proprietor.

Apparently, in another ironic twist of fate, Gene Chatsfield currently resided in the Chatsfield New York, leaving his new and highly acclaimed CEO, Christos Giatrakos, alone to handle operations from London. However, Gene Chatsfield's arrival in London to *personally* oversee the emir's visit said it all.

Knowing how key this high-profile guest's stay was to her father, Liyah was determined to do her job well. When she made herself known to Gene, there would be nothing to disappoint him in *her* work ethic.

Her floor was in impeccable order, each of the rooms to be occupied garnished with a crystal bowl of fruit and a vase of fragrant jasmine. She'd arranged for a screen to be placed at the elevator bank on her floor, as well, effectively blocking the harem quarters from curious looks.

She'd made sure the sheikh's suite was similarly taken care of. There was nothing to offend and a great deal to appreciate in her setup of his rooms and the floor below.

Thoughts of her work faded as an older man walked with supreme confidence across the lobby. His air that of a man who owned all he surveyed, he acknowledged the numerous greetings by his employees with a regal tip of his head. Her father.

Stopping in front of the reception desk, he was clearly prepared to welcome the sheikh upon arrival.

Gray hair shot with silver, his blue eyes were still clear, his six-foot-one frame just slightly stooped. Garbed in a perfectly tailored Pierre Cardin suit, his shoes no doubt handmade, he looked like a man who would fit right in with the fabulously wealthy people his hotel catered to.

Gene smiled and said something to the head of desk reception. And all the air expelled from Liyah's lungs in a single whoosh.

She'd seen that smile in the mirror her whole life.

His lips were thinner, but the wide smile above a slightly pointed chin? That was so familiar it made her heart ache.

His eyes were blue, hers were green—but their shape was the same. That hadn't been obvious in the publicity shots she'd seen of him.

She'd gotten her mother's honey-colored skin, oval face, small nose and arched brows, not to mention Hena's black hair and five-foot-five stature. Their mother-daughter connection had been obvious to anyone who saw them together.

Liyah had never considered she might also share physical traits with her father.

The resemblance wasn't overly noticeable by any means, but that smile? Undeniably like hers.

This man was her father.

Hit with the profundity of the moment, Liyah's knees went to jelly and she had to put her hand against the wall for stability.

Unaware of her father's moderate financial support and way too aware of the Amari rejection of any connection, Liyah had spent her life knowing of only one person in her family.

Hena Amari.

Her mom was the only Amari who had ever recognized Liyah as a member of that family. A family who had cast her out for her *disgrace*.

And since her mom's death, Liyah had been alone. In that moment, she realized that if this man accepted her—even into the periphery of his life—she wouldn't be alone any longer.

Her father's face changed, the smile shifting to something a lot tenser than the expression he'd worn only seconds before. He stood a little straighter, his entire demeanor more alert.

Liyah's gaze followed his, and for the second time in as many minutes she went weak in the knees.

Surrounded by an impressive entourage and dressed in the traditional garb of a Zeena Sahran sheikh stood the most beautiful man Liyah had ever seen. Known for his macho pursuits and outlook, despite his supreme political diplomacy, the emir wouldn't appreciate the description, she was sure.

But regardless of…or maybe *because of* his over-six-foot height, square jaw and neatly trimmed, close-cropped facial hair, the sheikh's masculine looks carried a beauty she'd never before encountered.

No picture she'd ever seen did him justice. Two-dimensional imagery could never catch the reality of Sheikh Sayed bin Falah al Zeena's presence. Not his gorgeous looks or the leashed power that crackled in the air around him like electricity.

Nothing about the unadorned black *abaya* worn over Armani, burgundy *keffiyeh* on his head and black triple-stranded *egal* holding it in place expressed anything but conservative control. The Zeena Sahran color of royalty of the *keffiyeh* and three strands of the *egal,* rather than the usual two, subtly indicated his status as emir.

Wearing the traditional robe over a tailored designer suit with the head scarf implied supreme civilization.

And yet, to her at least, it was obvious the blood of desert warriors ran in his veins.

The first melech of Zeena Sahra had won independence for his tribe—which later became the founding people of the emirate of Zeena Sahra—through bloody battles western history books often glossed over.

Inexplicably and undeniably drawn to the powerful man, Liyah's feet carried her forward without her conscious thought or volition. It was only when she stood mere feet from the royal sheikh that Liyah came to an abrupt, embarrassed stop.

It was too late, though.

Sheikh Sayed's espresso-brown gaze fell on her and remained, inquiry evident in the slight quirking of his brows.

Considered unflappable by all who knew her, Liyah couldn't think of a single coherent thing to say, not even a simple welcome before moving on.

No, she stood there, her body reacting to his presence in a way her mother had always warned Liyah about but she had never actually experienced.

Part of her knew that he was surrounded by the people traveling with him, the Chatsfield Hotel staff and even her father, but Liyah could only see the emir. Discussion around them was nothing more than mumbling to her ears.

The signature scent of the Chatsfield—a mix of cedarwood, leather, white rose and a hint of lavender—faded and all she could smell was the emir's spicy cologne blending with his undeniable masculine scent.

Her nipples drew tight for no discernible reason, her

heart rate increasing like it only did after a particularly challenging workout and her breath came in small gasps she did her best to mask with shallow inhales.

His expression did not detectably change, but something in the depths of his dark gaze told her she was not the only one affected.

"Sheikh al Zeena, this is Amari, our chambermaid floor supervisor in charge of the harem floor and your suite," the head of desk reception stepped in smoothly to say.

Being referred to by her last name was something Liyah was used to; meeting a crown prince was not.

However, her brain finally came back online and she managed to curl her right hand over her left fist and press them over her left breast. Bowing her head, she leaned slightly forward in a modified bow. "Emir. It is my pleasure to serve you and your companions."

Sayed had a wholly unacceptable and unprecedented reaction to the lovely chambermaid's words and actions.

His sex stirred, images of exactly *how* he would like her to serve him flashing through his mind in an erotic slide show of fantasies he was not aware of even having.

The rose wash over her cheeks and vulnerable, almost hungry expression in her green eyes told him those desires could be met, increasing his unexpected viscerally sexual reaction tenfold. Hidden by the fall of his *abaya,* his rapidly engorging flesh ached with unfamiliar need.

Sayed's status as a soon-to-be-married man, not to mention melech of his country, dictated he push the images aside and ignore his body's physical response, however. No matter how difficult he found doing so.

"Thank you, Miss Amari," Sayed said, his tone imperious by necessity to hide his reaction to her. He indicated the woman assigned to tend his domestic needs. "This is Abdullah-Hasiba. She will let you know of any requirements we may have. Should you have any questions, they can be taken directly to her, as well."

Miss Amari's beautiful green gaze chilled and her full lips firmed slightly, but nothing else in her demeanor indicated a reaction to his clear dismissal.

"Thank you, Your Highness." Dipping her head again in the tradition of his people, she then turned to his servant. "I look forward to working with you, Miz Abdullah-Hasiba."

With another barely there dip of her head, the much-too-attractive hotel employee did that thing well-trained servants were so good at and seemed to just melt away.

Sayed had a baffling and near-unstoppable urge to call her back.

HARLEQUIN®

Presents®

Harlequin Presents stories are all about romance and escape—glamorous settings, gorgeous women and the passionate, sinfully tempting men who want them.

From brooding billionaires to untamed sheikhs and forbidden royals, Harlequin Presents offers you the world!

Eight new passionate reads are available every month wherever books and ebooks are sold.

SPECIAL EXCERPT FROM

HARLEQUIN®

Presents

Harlequin Presents welcomes you to the world of
The Chatsfield:

Synonymous with style, spectacle...and scandal!

*Read on for an exclusive extract from Melanie Milburne's
sparkling story in this exciting eight-book series:*
PLAYBOY'S LESSON

* * *

CHARLOTTE's hand fluttered like a little bird inside the cage
of his, sending a shock wave of heat through his pelvis like
the back draft of a fire. Lucca released her hand and had to
physically stop himself from wriggling his fingers to rid
himself of the electric tingling her touch had evoked.

"Thank you, Your Royal Highness," he said with exagger-
ated politeness. He might be an irascible rake but he knew
how to behave when the occasion called for it, even if he pri-
vately thought it was all complete and utter nonsense. In his
opinion people were people. Rich or poor. Royal or common.

She pressed her lips together so tightly, as if she were trying to hold an invisible piece of paper between them steady.
He wasn't sure if it was out of annoyance or a gesture of
nervousness or shyness, but it drew his gaze like starving
eyes to a feast. She had a bee-stung mouth, full-lipped and
rosy-pink without the adornment of lipstick or even a layer
of clear lip gloss. It was a mouth that looked capable of intense passion, but it seemed somewhat at odds with the rest
of her downplayed and rather starchily set features.

A feather of intrigue tickled Lucca's interest. Did she have
a wild side behind those frumpy clothes and that frosty facade?

Maybe his exile here wouldn't be a complete waste of time after all….

She stepped back from him like someone would do in front of a suddenly too-hot fire. She squared her slim shoulders and crossed her hands over the front of her body, cupping her elbows with the opposite hands. "I believe you have been appointed as my assistant."

Lucca was seriously getting off on her priggish hauteur. It was so different from the way women usually responded to him. There was no simpering and batting of eyelashes. No breathy coos and whispers. No coy come-hither looks or pouting lips and delectable cleavages on show.

No, sirree.

She was buttoned up to the neck and spoke to him in clipped formal sentences while looking at him down the length of her retroussé nose as if he was something unpleasant stuck to the sole of her sensible shoe.

"That's correct." He gave her a mocking at-your-service bow.

Her chin came up a little higher and those striking eyes flashed like green-tinged lightning behind those conservative spectacle frames. "I think you should know that your appointment is both unnecessary and expressly against my wishes."

Wow. Now that was some attitude.

He'd had every intention of leaving her to it but something about her stiff unfriendliness irked him. He wasn't used to being dismissed as if he was nothing more than a lowly ranked servant who had failed to come up to scratch. He was an heir of one of the richest families in England. He decided to dig his heels in. He wasn't going to let some hoity-toity little princess rob him of his allowance by dismissing him before he'd put in a day's "work." He would play the game for the sake of appearances and keep everybody at home happy.

"Your sister's wedding cannot go ahead without my family's cooperation," he said. "The Chatsfield Hotel is the only venue large and modern enough in Preitalle to accommodate a royal wedding reception."

She gave him a defiant stare. "We can have it here at the palace ballroom. It's what I proposed to my sister in the first place."

"But that's not what your sister wants," he countered neatly. It felt like a verbal fencing match and just as stimulating. He could feel the stirring of his blood, like a tapping beat picking up its tempo, taking heat to his groin like a spreading fire. "The hotel is closer to the cathedral, and she wants the neutral ground of The Chatsfield to show how forward-thinking the royal house of Preitalle is becoming, does she not?"

Her lips compressed again. He could almost hear the cogs of her smart little brain ticking over. She was planning a counterattack. He could see the flickering behind her eyes as if she was mentally shuffling through her storehouse of comments to choose the most waspish one to send his way. "I fail to see how a man who spends his life frittering away his time and his family's money on a profligate lifestyle such as yours could have anything to offer me in terms of services."

Lucca smiled a satirical smile. "Au contraire, little princess. I think I have just the services you need."

* * *

*Step into the gilded world of **THE CHATSFIELD!***
Where secrets and scandal lurk behind every door…

Reserve your room!
May 2014

HP132393